She doesn't just walk through her front door.

That would be too easy.

She built a house where she could climb over the roof first!

LITTLE MISS SOMERSAULT

Roger Hargreaves

Original concept by
Roger Hargreaves

EGMONT

Little Miss Somersault is the sort of a person who doesn't just go out for a walk.

Oh no, not Little Miss Somersault.

She is too full of energy for that.

Rather than walking everywhere, she cartwheels everywhere!

Little Miss Somersault doesn't just sit in a chair.

She balances on the back of it.

Little Miss Somersault doesn't walk around things.

She jumps right over them!

And rather than answer the telephone as you or I might, she …

… well, just look at her!

The other day, when she was cartwheeling past Mr Worry's house, he called out to her.

"There's a leaf on my roof. Please could you get it for me?" he asked.

Mr Worry had spent the whole morning worrying that the leaf might make his roof fall in!

"I have a long ladder," he added.

Little Miss Somersault said, "I don't need a ladder."

And, quick as a flash, she climbed on top of Mr Worry's house and got the leaf off.

A little further down the lane, Little Miss Somersault came to Mr Skinny's house.

Mr Skinny was at the top of a ladder, painting his roof.

Unfortunately, Mr Bump came round the corner and walked under the ladder.

Or rather, he tried to walk under the ladder but, being Mr Bump, he walked straight into it.

BUMP!

And you can see what happened!

Little Miss Somersault had seen it all happen.

And, without a thought for the ladder lying on the ground, she climbed to the top of Mr Skinny's house and carried him safely to the ground.

Under her arm!

He wasn't very heavy!

By the next morning everybody had heard about Little Miss Somersault's daring deeds.

The telephone rang. It was Mr Uppity.

"There's an umbrella stuck in my chimney. I hear you're good at climbing on to roofs. I'll expect you here in five minutes!"

Mr Uppity's house is one of the biggest houses you will ever have seen.

"To climb to the top of Mr Uppity's house would be a real challenge," said Little Miss Somersault.

It took no time at all for Little Miss Somersault to climb on to Mr Uppity's roof.

"That was easy," she said, as she balanced on a chimney pot.

Then she looked down at the ground, far below her.

That was the last thing she should have done.

Little Miss Somersault suddenly felt dizzy.

Her knees began to tremble.

Everything began to spin round and round.

Little Miss Somersault had discovered she was afraid of heights!

Luckily, Mr Tickle happened to be passing.

He stretched out one of his extraordinarily long arms.

Do you think he wanted to tickle Little Miss Somersault?

Of course he did!

But not before he had brought her back safely down
to the ground.

"Stop it!" laughed Little Miss Somersault. "I promise
I won't do anything so foolish again!"

And off went Mr Tickle to look for somebody else
to tickle.

That evening Little Miss Somersault was sitting, that's right, sitting, in her armchair.

Suddenly, the telephone rang.

"My hat has blown off," said a voice at the other end. "And it's landed on the roof of my house. Could you …"

Little Miss Somersault's face turned pale.

"Who is this?" she asked, in a trembling voice.

"It's Mr Small," said Mr Small.

Little Miss Somersault breathed a huge sigh of relief.

"I'll be there in five minutes!" she said.

And off she somersaulted!